This edition published by Parragon Books Ltd in 2017 and distributed by

Parragon Inc.
440 Park Avenue South, 13th Floor
New York, NY 10016
www.parragon.com

ISBN 978-1-4748-8317-7

Printed in China

ALICE
in
WONDERLAND

MAGICAL STORY
COLLECTION

Bath • New York • Cologne • Melbourne • Delhi
Hong Kong • Shenzhen • Singapore

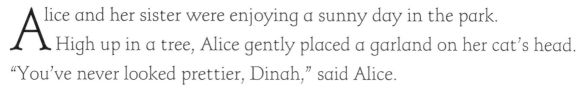

Alice and her sister were enjoying a sunny day in the park.
High up in a tree, Alice gently placed a garland on her cat's head.
"You've never looked prettier, Dinah," said Alice.

Her sister read out a lesson from a book.
But the day was far too lovely for learning!
"In my world, there would be no classes,"
Alice told Dinah. "Everything would be nonsense."

In the summer heat, Alice's eyelids grew heavy. She began
to fall asleep, when suddenly . . . a White Rabbit ran by.

Alice scrambled out of the tree and raced after him.

"He must be going somewhere important, like a party,"
she told Dinah.

He was heading toward a rabbit hole.

Alice squeezed into the rabbit hole to
follow the rabbit. Though she knew that curiosity
often leads to . . .

. . . "TROUBBBBLLLE!" Alice disappeared
into a dark hole.

The rabbit hole turned into a bright tunnel filled with strange objects.

Alice kept falling … down,
down,
down, until she landed with
a bump and chased the rabbit down a hallway.

"Oh, wait, Mr. Rabbit, please!" Alice called, as the rabbit ran down the hallway.

Slam! The White Rabbit pulled a door shut behind him.

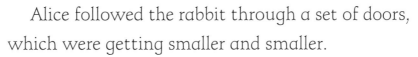

Alice followed the rabbit through a set of doors,
which were getting smaller and smaller.

"Curiouser and curiouser," Alice said.

She arrived at a tiny door and twisted the knob.
A nose wriggled under her hand!

Alice asked if she could go through.

"Sorry," said the Doorknob. "You're too big."

"Why don't you try the bottle on the table?"
the Doorknob suggested.

A glass bottle labeled "Drink Me" appeared.

With each sip, Alice shrank smaller and smaller and smaller.
Now she could fit through the door. But the door was locked
and she had left the key on top of the table, which was now
far above her head.

She ate a magic cookie that made her big again.
Too big to fit through the door.

Alice began to cry, and her tears flooded the room.
She took another sip from the bottle and she shrank
down so small that she fell into the empty bottle. It
floated on her tears through the door's keyhole.

On the other side of the door was
a huge ocean.

A big wave washed Alice onto the shore.
There were strange animals everywhere!
Suddenly, Alice spotted the White Rabbit.
"Mr. Rabbit!" she cried.

Alice chased the White Rabbit
until she was deep in a forest.
There, she met a pair of twins.
"I'm Tweedledee," said one.
"I'm Tweedledum," said the other.

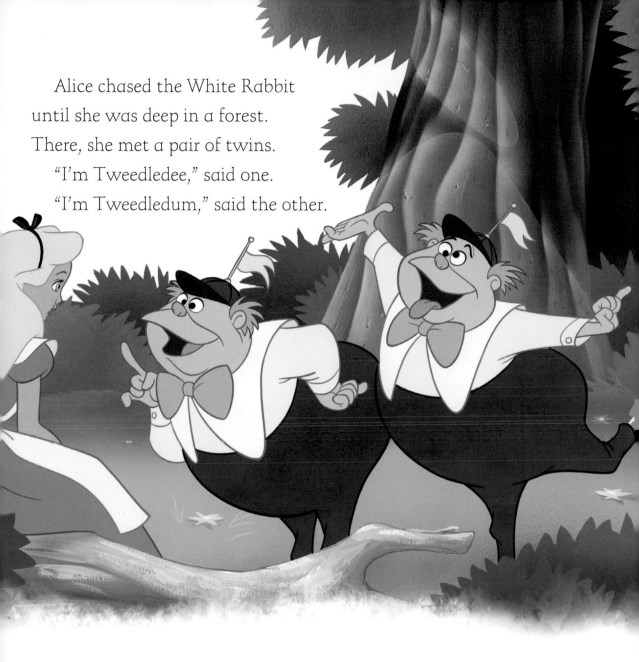

Alice told them that she was following the White Rabbit.
"I'm curious to know where he's going," she said.
"Being curious can often lead to trouble," Tweedledum said.

But Alice was still desperate to find the White Rabbit.
She hurried after him and arrived at a pretty cottage.
The White Rabbit rushed out.
"I'm late!" he cried. "Go and get my gloves!"

Inside his cottage, Alice found cookies labeled "Eat Me". Alice happily helped herself.

Soon she felt herself growing . . . and growing . . . until her arms and legs stuck out of the cottage windows!

"HELP! It's a monster!" the White Rabbit cried.

Alice ate a carrot from the White Rabbit's garden and shrank back down again to her tiny size.

But the White Rabbit was already racing away.

"Oh dear," said tiny Alice. "I'll never catch him!"

Alice followed him into a forest, but she
couldn't tell which way to go.

She heard singing and gazed up into a tree. A
Cheshire Cat with a huge, wide mouth grinned
back at her.

"If you'd like to know," the cat said,
"the White Rabbit went that way."

Alice walked until she heard more singing.

It was the Mad Hatter and the March Hare.

They were having a tea party.

Alice tried to join them, but the pair shouted,

"No room!"

The Mad Hatter swept off his hat and wished
Alice a "merry unbirthday".
There, on top of his head, was an unbirthday cake!
"Now blow out the candle and make your wish," said
the Mad Hatter.

As if in answer to Alice's wish, the White Rabbit appeared. "I'm late!" he cried.

The Mad Hatter and the March Hare decided that the rabbit's watch was broken. That's why he was always late.

They fixed it with jam and lemon!

By now, Alice was tired of this nonsense.

In the trees above her, Alice heard the Cheshire Cat again.

"I want to go home," she told him.

The Cheshire Cat opened a door in the tree.

Alice stepped through it, into the world of the Queen of Hearts.

The White Rabbit raced into the royal court.

This was why he was in such a rush.

He didn't want to be late to meet the queen.

"Her Imperial Highness!" called
the White Rabbit. "The Queen of Hearts!"
The courtiers cheered as the queen entered.

The queen spotted Alice.
"Why, it's a little girl! Where are
you from and where are
you going?"

"I'm trying to find my way home,"
Alice told her.
"Your way?" the queen cried.
"All ways here are my ways!"

Alice played a game of croquet with the
queen, but it ended badly. The queen became
angry when their game was ruined.

Alice was sent to court.

"Off with her head!" said the queen.

Her guards, shaped like playing cards,
closed in around Alice.

But she managed to escape and raced away.

As Alice ran, she saw the door she had gone through earlier.
Alice tugged on the Doorknob.

"I must get out!" she gasped.

"But you are outside," the Doorknob said.

Alice peered through the keyhole.

There she was, sleeping in the meadow!

"Alice!" Alice's sister woke her. "It's time for tea."

Sleepily, Alice looked around. Her wonderland was gone. The angry queen had disappeared.

Alice shook away her dream and smiled.

It was a lovely summer's day. Too lovely for nonsense!